PINGU

Does the Housework

BBC CHiLDRENS BOOKS

All was quiet in Pingu's house. Mum was hard at work ironing, Pingu was reading a book and Pinga was playing with her toys.

Mum looked up from her ironing and sighed wearily. The house was in a terrible mess. She would never get it all cleared up before Dad came home. And she felt *so* tired today.

She looked across at Pingu and suddenly felt cross. "Come and help me, Pingu," she called. "I've got such a lot of housework to be getting on with and all you can do is sit there reading that book."

"Why can't Pinga help you?" said Pingu. "She's only playing with her toys. And anyway, you like tidying up, don't you, Pinga?"

"Oh, yes please, Mum," said Pinga. "I love helping."

"You're much too small," said Mum.

"No, I'm not," said Pinga and she reached up for the pile of clothes Mum had just ironed.

On her way over to the cupboard Pinga dropped some of the clothes.

"I've just washed and ironed those and now they're all dirty and crumpled again," snapped Mum.

Pinga burst into tears. "I was only trying to help," she sobbed.

"I'm sorry I was cross," said Mum gently. "I know you couldn't help it. I just feel very tired today."

Pingu saw Mum coming towards him and he hid behind his book.

"It's no good pretending you're not there, Pingu," said Mum. "You're bigger than Pinga and you'll just have to help me."

Mum gave Pingu a large pile of clothes to put
away. Pingu balanced them on his head and danced
about as he made his way over to the cupboard.
  "Do be careful!" cried Mum.

Pingu was soon back reading his book again. But not for long.

"Pingu!" called out Mum. "I haven't finished with you yet. Come here at once. There's work to be done!"

Pingu groaned.

"You can clean the floor now," said Mum.

"No, I can't," said Pingu. "I'm much too small."

"Nonsense!" said Mum.

12

Suddenly, Pingu began to cheer up. While Mum's back was turned he tipped lots more soap powder into the water. He laughed to himself as the bucket filled with bubbles.

"Yippee!" cried Pinga. "I love bubbles!"
"Good!" laughed Pingu as he plopped a huge
handful of them on her head.

"Mum, Mum," cried Pinga, rushing over to Mum's side. "Look what Pingu's done."

Mum rubbed the bubbles off Pinga's head. "Stop being silly and just get on with the cleaning, Pingu," she said in a tired voice.

While Mum went outside to see if the washing was dry, Pingu discovered what fun he could have playing ice-hockey with the cloth.

"Watch out!" he yelled at Pinga, hitting the soggy cloth up into the air. It struck the wall with a thud.

Mum came back inside to find Pingu and Pinga giggling.

"And just what do you think you're doing?" she shouted. "You're supposed to be helping me, not making more work. Pingu, come with me and fetch the washing in this instant."

Pinga decided to try and clean the floor all by herself. What a nice surprise she would give Mum. But when she lifted up the broom she knocked a clean bedspread right into the bucket of soapy water.

"Oh, no!" she cried, fishing out the wet bedspread. "What will Mum say?" Then she had an idea.

She took the bedspread over to the oven and popped it inside. "It should dry quickly in there," she said to herself.

After a while, Pingu and Mum came inside with the clean washing. Before Mum could ask Pingu to do anything else he slipped quickly back to his book.

"I give up," sighed Mum.

At last the housework was finished and it was time to get the supper. Mum stirred the fish stew in the saucepan. She felt much happier now that the house was clean and tidy.

Pingu was laying the table. He like doing this much more than cleaning the floor.

Just then Dad came back from work.

"I'm home!" he called out cheerfully, as he hung his bag and Post Office hat on a peg.

"Dad!" shrieked Pinga happily, giving him a big hug.

"Hello, little Pinga," said Dad. "I hope you've been a good girl today."

Dad went and gave Mum a kiss. "Have you had a good day?" he asked.

"I've been very busy with the housework," said Mum. "But Pingu has helped me."

Pingu puffed himself up proudly. "I worked very hard," he told Dad.

"Well done, Pingu," said Dad. "I'm sure you were a great help."

Mum opened the door of the oven and was very shocked to find her best bedspread cooking away inside it.

"Oh, my goodness!" she exclaimed. "What is that doing in here? It could have caught fire and burnt the house down!"

"Who put the bedspread in there?" asked Dad, looking at Pingu.

"It wasn't me, honestly," said Pingu. "I know how dangerous that could be."

Pinga hid nervously behind her brother and said nothing.

Pingu went up to the bedspread and hugged it.
"Mmmm," he said. "It feels lovely and warm. Can
we have it on our bed tonight?"
Mum and Dad smiled at him.

That night, Pingu and Pinga were tucked up in bed under the burnt bedspread.

"You shouldn't have put it in the oven, Pinga, but I do like it better with holes in it," said Pingu. "And anyway, after all the housework I've done today I could fall asleep under anything!"

Published by BBC Children's Books
a division of BBC Worldwide Limited
Woodlands, 80 Wood Lane, London W12 0TT
First published 1996

ISBN 0 563 40444 2

Typeset by BBC Children's Books
Colour separations by DOT Gradations, Chelmsford
Printed and bound by Cambus Litho, East Kilbride